The Kr

The Knell Gate

The curfew tolls the knell of parting day
Beneath those rugged elms, that yew trees shade
Where heaves the turf in many a mouldering heap
Each in his narrow cell forever laid
The rude forefathers of the hamlet sleep

(Thomas Gray 1716-71)

E.J.P. HESLOP

© E.J.P. Heslop, 2023

Published by Wilkinson Publishing

Disclaimer
All characters in this book are fictitious, any resemblance to any person or place in this work is purely coincidental.

A CIP catalogue record for this book is available from the British Library.

ISBN 978-1-7390845-0-9

Book layout and cover design by Clare Brayshaw
© Illustration 171119716 © obsidianfantasy |
Dreamstime.com

Prepared and printed by:

York Publishing Services Ltd
64 Hallfield Road
Layerthorpe
York YO31 7ZQ

Tel: 01904 431213

Website: www.yps-publishing.co.uk

Hurworth Parish Council

Knell Gate

During the plague, bodies from nearby villages
were ferried across the River Tees.
This passageway linked the river to the Green.
Once at the gate, a bell was rung to warn
villagers to go inside their houses.
Knell means bell.

Dedicated to the beautiful village of Hurworth.
To residents, past and present.
For the seventy five survivors of the 1665
plague, who re- built the community,

"Thank You"

CHAPTER 1

The Village

Hurworth is a large village, nestling on the banks of the river Tees, not what you would call a sleepy village, more vibrant than that.

Surrounded by other smaller villages, such as Croft, Eryholme, and Girsby to name but a few, all ancient with their own fascinating histories.

Large period houses surround the village green in Hurworth leading on to the beautiful church of All Saints.

There are three pubs, a small supermarket and a fish and chip shop.

Within the village, what was St Cuthbert's Hospital, run by the Brothers from the Hospitallers of St John of God, is now a stunning five star hotel complex, with a championship golf course, Middlesbrough Football Club have their training ground there and the state of art sports facilities are second to none.

There is a community centre, Hurworth Grange, built and gifted as a wedding present by Alfred Backhouse to his nephew.

Following residential use, the Brothers of St John of God used it in the Nineteen fifties as a school for boys wishing to become Hospitaller Brothers.

Durham Count Council purchased The Grange in 1968, and despite lucrative bids from developers; it was then given to Hurworth Parish Council.

A wonderful venue for many community occasions.

In the 17th Century, the great plague swept across the nation leaving many towns and villages desolated, not differentiating between rich and poor, it affected everyone in some way. Hurworth was no different. In 1665, the plague hit Hurworth. Of the population of c.750, only 75 survived. Today, you can see three depressions on the village green that mark the site of huge lime pits, in which up to 1500 people were believed to be buried in. People from the surrounding villages as well as Hurworth. Whose bodies would be ferried from across the Tees and buried there.

It is believed that a bell would toll as the bodies were carried up the lane to the village green, warning anyone in earshot to stay clear.

CHAPTER 2

"The Emmy"

Our story begins in one of the local pubs, The Emerson Arms affectionately known as "The Emmy", named after mathematician William Emerson who resided in a house on the village green. He was born in 1701, and died in 1782, his gravestone in All Saints Church is written in Latin and Hebrew.

The Emmy, overlooks the river Tees and the striking countryside beyond,

Many patrons have been coming for years, watching the view change with the seasons, sitting outside on the terrace on warm days and evenings, or indoors perched on tall bar stools, still mesmerised by the amazing vista.

Topics of conversation are always interesting, sometimes serious, and sometimes jovial but always welcoming.

December 2019

Friday evening, the usual crowd are perched around the noisy back bar, noise levels as usual are high and jovial, most are discussing plans for Christmas, which is fast approaching, tickets for the village hall quiz already sold out. The tree is up and lit on the green, ready for the annual outdoor carol service.

There will be the usual Christingle in the church, with little ones allowed to call in the pub afterwards with mums and dads, clutching the treasured orange with candle.

Tom and Ellen have lived in the village for over 40 years, and the traditions seldom change, their sons are now grown and married, like many of the other regular's families, but most of them find their way back at this special time.

Annie and Charles are relatively newcomers, only living in in Hurworth for a mere 15 years, Henry and Suzanna 30 years and Michael and Isabel who are both in their 90s have been here all their lives, both fit and well, enjoying the company of the younger ones, they always have many tales of times gone by, and how things were "back in the day". They were great friends of Toms father, and when Tom was young his father would bring him from town to visit them, they were like an Aunt and Uncle to him, his love of the village grew from those visits and when the time came to settle down, there was only one place he wanted to be.

After a few glasses of red wine, Michael would always embarrass Tom by recalling events when he was a youngster, like the time he was not quite four and when sitting on a bench at the edge of the village green, Michael read out the plaque remembering all the people who had died during the plague in 1665, Tom had commented that they weren't dead, but running around under the grass, he said he saw men fighting with swords and hammers and the children joining hands and singing ring a roses. Michael had thought nothing of it at the time.

Tom and Michael are discussing food, Friday is usually fish and chip night, but Toms' son Sam, is visiting and has requested Chinese takeaway.

The conversation leads to a current random news story, stating that a virus has been discovered in Wuhan China; apparently the source is suspected to be a food market selling meat and fish.

"Sounds like that 'SARS'" says Tom, yes agrees Michael, although there is a research laboratory close by which is being investigated apparently.

As the night draws to a close the bar starts to empty and all thoughts turn to tasty suppers, any talk of viruses are soon forgotten.

January 2020

Cases of the new virus are rising; there is an uneasy air throughout as news filters through to the West.

835 have now been confirmed in China, also other countries are also recording an increase in levels, it is now indicated that the virus can be transmitted from human to human.

In the following months it is apparent that the world is experiencing a pandemic.

In the UK cases were rising daily and the death rate increasing at an alarming rate, as with the 1665 plague, covid did not differentiate between old, young, rich, poor, all were affected.

York England
29th January 2020

First UK cases of covid 19 reported in York, a Chinese student and his mother who had just flown in from Wuhan a week earlier, the student rang 111; describing symptoms of dry cough and sore throat.

They were taken to a specialist hospital in Newcastle.

March 23rd 2020
Lock Down

Everyone knew it was coming, but The Prime Minister has officially announced that the country is to lock down; all pubs, restaurants and non-essential shops were to close.

Hurworth itself has not been affected too badly with covid, but unease is with everyone.

Even though Tom has been feeling under the weather lately, he and Ellen decide to have one last drink in the Emmy, not knowing what the future holds, they meet up with all the usual crowd, all are cautious, payment at the bar is card only, people are touching elbows, none of the usual hugs.

Folk start to drift home, Tom and Ellen prepare to leave, Tom a bit worse for wear, even though he has only had the usual couple of pints of Guinness, tells Ellen, "you put tea on I'm going to walk long way round to clear my head."

He walks on towards the green, for March it is still chilly, snowdrops and aconites line the edges of the path, with a mist lowering quickly, his head is fuzzy and he thinks he hears horses and a bell somewhere, he pulls up his collar, and then gradually starts to fall, the mist envelopes him into the darkness.

CHAPTER 3

Hunworth – March 23rd 1665

Thomas pulls up his collar against the cold March wind, he has just left the alehouse, as the village smithy, he often calls there after a long day working at his anvil. His work is hard, and lately because of the illness, more and more gentry are moving out of the big towns like York, and taking up residence at the big house, they bring with them horses, carriages and carts, which all need to be maintained, Thomas already does all the iron work for the big house, his son Samuel is a strong boy of eighteen years now and works along side his father.

The earlier mist has cleared but he strides on past the village green, towards the cottage, where Eleanor will be waiting with a pan of warm pottage on the blazing fire, with any luck, Samuel will have been given a pigs trotter by cook at the big house.

As he approaches the school house he rushes past the lane that leads down to the river, he has only heard the Knell toll once since the start of the sickness, the bell that sounds the arrival of bodies from surrounding villages to be buried on the green, there is already one mound, surrounded by snowdrops and aconites, naturally honouring the bodies beneath.

There is now much talk of the sickness spreading at a fast rate.

The Big House

The big house, is set back on the riverbank, a large elegant property, with stunning gardens leading down to the river, surrounded by fields and woodland.

His Lordship is a kindly gentleman, who helps the village community by employing as many as possible to work the land and keep the house in order. He is a widower, his wife died giving birth to their youngest daughter Elizabeth 16 years ago, he also has a son of eighteen James, who has been at college in York, but has returned due to what is now known as The Plague.

Unlike the larger towns, most villages had closely knit communities when Samuel , Elizabeth and James were younger, they would spend most of their days exploring the vast woodlands around the big house, they would set off in the morning, armed with tasty bites from the kitchen, they had discovered a small shack which was owned by the Brothers on the edge of the village, they rarely saw the Brothers, but knew they were around to keep them from harm.

Elizabeth would pretend to set up home, and the boys would fish and swim in the river, returning to Elizabeth to share whatever cook had prepared for them, there was no thought of gentry or commoners, just a bond that they thought would last a lifetime.

Sadly, when James reached the age of twelve, he was sent to St Peters school in York as a boarder, he grew more and more distant especially from Samuel.

There were times when James would return for a weekend, and bring along friends from his new school, at first Samuel was allowed to join in their boisterous activities, as time went by, he became reluctant to go along to their shoots and fox hunts, especially when James expected him to cow tow to them and look after the dogs and guns.

Samuel watched as James changed, it saddened him, but knew that as heir to the Big House, the friendship they had for so long, could no longer be.

A governess at home then taught Elizabeth, and Samuel attended the schoolhouse in the village, the time soon came when he would leave and go to work with his father at the smithy.

His favourite job was to go with Thomas to the big house, and tend the horses there, he always managed to sneak off and catch up with Elizabeth, although they did not venture as far as the shack, they still spent many hours together, Elizabeth was growing into a beautiful young lady, Samuel knew eventually she would have to marry into a titled family, but for now they just enjoyed the innocence of their friendship.

March 1665

The big house is full of visitors, most from the larger towns and cities; it is known that King Charles has left London for Oxford. Parliament has also fled to Oxford, and the initial reaction was to ignore the first few cases, however it soon grew to unignorable proportions.

Eleanor has just finished her work in the large kitchen, and heads back home, her days are also longer now, but she has a good relationship with cook. A motherly figure who serves his Lordship and family well.

She pops her head round the stable door as she leaves, knowing that Samuel will be still working, she comes across Samuel and Elizabeth deep in conversation about the latest visitors, Elizabeth is wary of some of them, she is very protective of her father, and asks Samuel to be on his guard. Samuel agrees, with a cheeky grin, only a mother would know how smitten he is with this beautiful girl, but he can never have any chance of showing his emotions, Lords and Commoners don't mix.

Eleanor arrived back at the cottage to find Thomas deeply distressed, the old couple Michael and Isobel who live up the lane, both have contracted the sickness, a red cross has been painted on the door, ensuring no contact is made; he has been and left ale and bread outside.

He knows there is no cure for the sickness, and the symptoms are horrific, with chocking coughs, fever and terrible swellings, some people died within days of contracting the plague, and at over 80 years old, Thomas knew Michael and Isobel would be lucky to last the night.

His fears were confirmed, when early the next morning, he saw the church rector, leading the corpse bearer and his wagon of death, up to the village green, the bodies of the old couple were wrapped roughly in common shrouds, no coffins. Local men were waiting with heaps of lime to cover the bodies, hoping to prevent the disease spreading. His doleful cry of God Have Mercy Upon Us rang out over the hushed village.

The rector died but a few days later.

CHAPTER 4

Darlington Memorial – April 2020

Respiratory Ward

Tom lies motionless, attached to a ventilator, which breathes for him, he has been like this for four weeks now, since he was found at the edge of Hurworth Green one March evening.

The hospital is at full capacity, with staff working round the clock to cope with the ever-increasing stream of admissions.

Some are only here a few days, others much longer.

There is talk of a vaccine, but it could take years to develop.

No visitors are allowed, and Ellen can only keep in touch by telephone, the staff organise video calls, and encourage her to talk to him.

She tells him about the boys, and how Sam has a new job in York, he and his wife Liz, are expecting their first child.

The pandemic has touched everyone, something never seen in a lifetime, social distancing, panic buying, care homes with not enough specialist equipment to save the hundreds of vulnerable elderly.

Even their families are not allowed to visit, and many passed away without a loving hand to hold.

Throughout the pandemic, the NHS worked tirelessly, new hospitals were erected in weeks, the public responded by turning out every Wednesday evening to applaud them, in the village the sound of clapping could be heard loud and clear.

Travel is restricted, and any passengers arriving in the UK must isolate for 14 days.

By the end of June there had been 64.000 deaths related to covid in the UK alone.

Restrictions were starting to ease by the end of the month, and retailers were allowed to open, with strict rules on social distancing in place.

Early one morning, Ellen receives a call from the hospital, Tom is starting to stir, the ventilator has been removed, and he is delirious and is talking about bodies being placed in the ground.

"The cart, the cart", he is shouting, "keep away, keep away."

He falls back into his deep sleep, but the staff is convinced it is a good sign, and tell Ellen not to give up on him.

The weeks pass, with not much change, occasionally, Tom will stir and ramble about The Big House and for Sam to take care, only he calls him Samuel.

CHAPTER 5

Hunworth – July 1665

Ring a Ring of Roses

Ring a Ring of Roses
*(A ring of roses was the red rash often one of the
early signs of the plague)*
A pocket full of posies
*(Was thought to ward of the bad smells that
people thought were causing the plague)*
Atishoo, Atishoo
*(Sneezing and coughing was the final fatal
symptom of the plague)*
We all fall down
(Meant to mean falling down dead)

The mounds on the village green have increased
tenfold, most of the villagers have locked
themselves up in their houses, to try to avoid the
escalating contamination.

It has been weeks since Thomas and Samuel have been to the big house, which has also been locked up, with many of the residents now showing signs of the plague.

Eleanor has been covering herself in sacking, soaked with vinegar, she calls to help cook as much as she dare, but now realises with new cases every day that she can no longer continue.

Cook has packed her a basket of meat and vegetable and wishes her well.

Eleanor leaves with tears in her eyes, concerned about his Lordship and his son James and of course Elizabeth.

As she is leaving, Elizabeth rushes past the open kitchen door, Eleanor calls to her, "are you well Miss Elizabeth?"

Elizabeth carries on to the stables, Eleanor follows and at a distance cries, stop, as Elizabeth turns, it is obvious that she is with child.

Elizabeth falls to the ground sobbing, and tells Eleanor how James' friend from York, had forced himself upon her, he told her Father that it was her that had made advances.

The man in question was Jasper Fencote the son of a nobleman in York; he had arranged that they would be wed, as soon as it was safe to return to York. Elizabeth's father, although distraught at the situation his beautiful daughter was in, had no grounds to disbelieve the word of a gentleman.

Jasper and his brother were two of the only visitors remaining, too scared to venture out, or return to York where deaths were rising even more.

Eleanor motioned to Elizabeth, to try to stay calm, she advised her to stay indoors and away from everyone; she would ask Thomas how they could help.

When Eleanor returned home, Thomas and Samuel were digging the last of the spring vegetables; times were going to be hard, even if they did survive the plague.

She motioned to Thomas to come inside; he did leaving Samuel deep in his task.

She whispered to Thomas about Elizabeth, "what can we do to help the poor girl?" as she turned she saw Samuel in the doorway, his strong frame almost blocking the fading sunlight, he had heard her words, the rage in his eyes was something Eleanor had never seen before.

Picking up his hammer from the forge he strode towards the big house, Thomas called after him, but knew that he would not have the strength to stop him.

It was nearly dark when he arrived at the back of the stables of the big house, the candles were lit and fires were burning brightly. His Lordship sat in a winged back chair, his gaze, somewhere in a distant place.

James, Jasper and his brother Henry were standing by the fire wine glasses in hand, Elizabeth was nowhere to bee seen.

Samuel crept to where he knew Elizabeth's room was just above the ivy clad porch, he threw some pebbles at the window, no response, he tried again, just as he was about to give up hope, she came to the window,

Her face was gaunt, her beautiful hair tied back in a simple knot.

Samuel's heart missed a beat, "I know" he said, "I heard mother tell father what happened."

"Stay here for now; I will come back for you, I promise."

Samuel made his way to rear if the house, towards the stables, where Jasper and his brother had come to tend the horses, there were no stable lads now.

They had been drinking most of the evening, and were laughing and joking, "how's the little lady?" Jaspers brother snorted, Jasper laughed back saying, "she cares not for me at all, and will not look at me, but as soon as we get to York, she will learn who her master is."

Samuel had been quiet up until this point, but could not contain his rage any longer, he stepped out of the shadows into the light of the lamps around the stables, the horses reared at the movement, Jasper and his brother turned at the same time.

"Well if it isn't our blacksmith come to tend us again, good man, please bed down the horses and make sure all is well for the ride tomorrow."

"I have not come to tend you or your horses; you have wronged an innocent girl, and abused the hospitality of a kind and generous Lord."

Jasper laughed at this, saying "what has this to do with you, a dirty blacksmiths boy."

"I am no boy", said Samuel, raising the hammer in his right hand

At this Henry drew a dagger from his belt and lunged towards Samuel.

Samuel blocked his arm with the hammer in his right hand, and threw a wild punch with his strong left arm, which landed square on Henrys chin, knocking him out instantly.

Both men stood looking at the motionless body of Henry, Jasper threw a menacing glance at Samuel and proceeded to pull his sword from its scabbard at his side, roaring at Samuel as he moved toward him, without stopping to think, Samuel hurled the hammer, it cartwheeled through the air, Jasper was quick to react and turned swiftly, to avoid it, but not in time and the hammer hit him just beneath the skull on the back of his neck, he fell to the ground, his body twitching, and eyes starring wide open.

At this point Thomas crashed through the stable door, what have you done he cried.

"I didn't mean to kill him, just to frighten them."

"He's not dead" said Thomas, "but looks as though he cannot move a muscle."

"I will get help, but you must flee, no one will believe your word against theirs.

Go to the Brothers on the edge of the village, they will hide you until I can come for you."

Samuel did as Thomas asked, slowly Henry started to stir, Thomas, who was tending to Jasper, rose, but Henry dashed out before he could stop him.

Jasper was still alive but obviously paralysed, his eyes pleading with Thomas to help him.

Thomas dragged him onto a wooden rack from the stable and pulled him to the big house, his Lordship had heard the commotion and opened the large wooden door, without a word he motioned for Thomas to put Jasper in the hallway, Thomas did as he asked, his Lordship put an understanding hand on Thomas' shoulder, no words were needed. Thomas looked across the hallway to see James sitting in the shadows of the library, the tell -tale signs of dark circles round his eyes which stared empty and outward, large boils on his face, the retching cough and fever, the end was near.

Samuel made his way through the woods, to the edge of the village, across the river, where the order of Brothers lived, a large, simple dwelling place, with acres of land, the Brothers tended the land and grew crops and vegetables, which fed them and anyone in the area in need of help.

They had cows, pigs and sheep, Thomas and Samuel had spent many hours, helping them over the years, and had become great friends with them all.

They had seen Samuel grow from a cheeky toddler, to a fine young man, so there was no hesitation when he called on them.

He was guided to a small dwelling quite away from the main house, set back in the woods out of sight to anyone passing. They were obviously cautious, so kept a safe distance.

Water was brought from a natural Spa in the woods, known as The Stinking Pit, where farmers would bring their horses and cattle, the water was well known for its healing qualities, the Brothers used it in their potions and natural remedies, Samuel was asked to bathe from head to toe, they gave him a soap, which was made from herbs and tree bark.

His clothes were burnt and a simple robe given to replace them.

He was told to stay in the small shack; food and water were there for him.

Thomas approached the brother's house slowly, he stopped short and waved to the head of the order, "I will come for him soon", but was reassured that Samuel was quite safe, and for Thomas to return as the Brothers had heard the plague had reached the big house.

Thomas ran back but the sight that met him made his blood freeze.

The cart was being loaded with three shrouded bodies.

A large red cross was painted on the door, before being boarded securely.

Thomas could see his Lordship still inside, cook was in the kitchen as busy as ever and on looking up saw Elizabeth's face at the bedroom window.

CHAPTER 6

Darlington Memorial – June 2020

Tom is gaining strength every day, and despite his memory loss and vivid dreams, there is talk of him coming home.

The country is still in partial lock down

Sadly, the family now inform him that Michael and Isabel, their good friends from "The Emmy" both contracted Covid and passed away.

His son Sam and his daughter in law Liz, have settled into their new house in York, a small terraced house with a simple back yard.

Because of Covid restrictions, Liz has to attend all of her anti natal appointments alone; Sam cannot even attend for the first scan.

They are happy though, Sam works from home and Liz is furloughed from her teaching assistant job.

They video call regularly, but miss coming home at weekends for mums Sunday roast.

They are busy painting the small room that will be the nursery, pretty giraffes in neutral shades of creams and lemons, most of the furnishing have been bought online, sadly replacing the exciting shopping trips that would have been before the pandemic.

It is a worrying time for Sam and Liz, they know that there is a chance that they could contract covid, there have been some cases where both mum and baby have died. They stay indoors, only venturing out for a little exercise; all groceries are purchased on line and delivered to the door.

Restrictions are being slowly lifted, and families can meet up in small groups, but Sam decides to stay in York and not put his wife or baby in any danger.

CHAPTER 7

Spa Woods – August 1665

Samuel has been alone in the shack for some weeks now, he ventures out only to snare rabbits, or fish for trout in the river.

One day as he approaches his dwelling place, he hears movement from inside, cautiously he creeps around to the side window space, there inside is Elizabeth looking terrified, she looks up and the fear in her face leaves instantly, he rushes in, and without any thought of illness or sickness holds her close, she collapses into his arms.

The Brothers had gone to the big house, and cook was struggling, his Lordship had survived so far but needed constant caring.

So they had told Elizabeth of Samuels hiding place and she agreed to join him, they had cook prepare her as they had Samuel, she was bathed in the Spa waters and given clean garments, and she was to take nothing with her.

The baby would be due in a few months, Elizabeth told Samuel how the little form inside her would kick and move.

They had no idea what would happen when the baby came, but Samuel reassured her that he would be there and they would face it together.

They embraced for the first time, but it seemed as if they had been together forever.

They spent the time in the little shack, always aware of cleaning and using the herbs and water that the Brothers brought.

There was a large cat, living in the undergrowth outside, he kept away the rats, and was rewarded with trout heads, although would never come close enough for any kind of attention, he would growl at anyone approaching him. The days were growing colder as summer turned to autumn, but the shack was cosy with a log stove.

The last flowers of the Honeysuckle and wild roses, arched naturally around the windows.

The Brothers had started to leave extra supplies, and also little packages of essentials for when the baby came.

A tiny crib had been hewn out of a tree trunk, and beautifully carved, it was filled with the softest blankets and shawls made from sheep's wool, that had been hand woven as fine as silk.

Their days were filled with short walks where only local people knew.

They would sit on the riverbank, watching Kingfishers and Heron fish. An otter would come along daily, teaching this years pups to fish.

They found a spot where mushrooms grew under the oak trees, and the season provided many a tasty meal.

At night they would sit by the glowing fire, both quite happy to be there.

The Brothers brought up to date news of the village, his Lordship was holding his own, cook was still well, and Thomas and Isabelle were healthy.

Sadly though, many of the village and surrounding areas had perished.

There were less than 100 residents remaining in the village, which once had over 750.

Farmers struggled to reap the crops, even though everyone pulled together, it would be years before life would be as before the plague hit.

CHAPTER 8

Hurworth – 31st October 2020

Boris Johnson has spoken to the nation yet again, the easing of restrictions has not worked and as from this day, the country was to return to lock down, albeit not as strict as before.

Schools were to remain open, but people were advised to work from home where possible,

non-essential shops, bars and restaurants, leisure and entertainment venues were all to close until at least early December.

The NHS is struggling to cope with the ever-increasing numbers of Covid cases; the army has been deployed to build pop up hospitals within weeks.

Stay at home. Protect the NHS. And save lives.

Christmas was once again looking bleak, families were allowed to form a bubble with one other group, but many took to shielding to protect the elderly and vulnerable.

There was more talk of a vaccine being ready in early 2021, and people were advised to use self-testing kits, which were supplied by the NHS.

Sam and Liz, although excited about the new arrival coming in December, were very concerned, hospital staff tried to reassure them, but they took to the internet for information, as there were no anti natal classes or mother and father groups. Sam would be allowed in the delivery room, for the birth of the baby, they knew the little one was going to be a girl. Tom and Ellen kept in touch, and tried to reassure them that all would be well, but the thought of not seeing their first grandchild for who knows when, was so painful.

CHAPTER 9

Spa Woods – November 1665

It was a mild morning, and Samuel and Elizabeth were walking near the river, enjoying the clear crisp sunshine, the wood was a wash of autumn shades. They picked a few remaining blackberries.

In the distance they heard a strange sound, they fled for cover and watched as a coach pulled by two horses drove past, there had been few visitors to the area since the beginning of the plague.

Samuel told Elizabeth to go back to the shack, and he skirted round the outside of the wood towards the big house.

It took a while, but just as he arrived, he saw a the coach driver alight from his seat, the driver kept his distance and called out, cook came to the window, Samuel could not make out what was said, but saw his Lordship come to the window, they exchanged a few words, and Samuel saw his

Lordship gesture towards the green. The driver bowed his head in appreciation and returned to the coach.

As the coach began to slowly move away, Samuel could see someone inside.

The coach pulled up alongside the village green, the mounds now settling, with fewer burials every day .

Samuel kept behind the undergrowth and watched as a distinguished gentleman stepped slowly out of the coach, he knew at once it was the father of Jasper Fencote.

The man looked solemnly at the site in front of him, his head bowed he wiped the tears from his eyes.

At that moment, the rumbling of the death cart pulled up the lane from the river; the ford crossing from the villages beyond was the pathway to the green.

The Knell bell tolled quietly, and the cart pulled up on the opposite side to where Jaspers father stood, the workers removed only one body from the cart, and placed it in the prepared open ground, the body was wrapped in sacking, and the form, showed a young mother and her new-born, tightly wrapped together, they were covered in lime, before the earth was piled on top.

One of the workers picked a small posy of Michaelmas daisies, from the hedgerow and placed them on the mound.

Jaspers father stood very still for quite a while then walked slowly back to the waiting coach, one more backward glance and he climbed inside.

Samuel could not hold his emotion, he still did not know whether it was he or the plague that had taken Jaspers life, but his heart went out to this father who grieved his son.

He imagined his own parents, standing there grieving.

He looked down the lane past the village green, to the cottage next to the smithy where his mother and father were, he wanted more than anything to run to the sanctuary of them and the place he grew up in, he hadn't seen them for months, but knew it would be too dangerous to make contact now.

The coach pulled away and Samuel started to walk back to the river and the comfort of his hide out, when he arrived he broke down Elizabeth held him so close, she would ask him tomorrow what had occurred, but for now they sat in silence, watching the flames of the fire light up the darkening room.

CHAPTER 10

York – November 2020

Sam and Liz take their daily walk in the afternoons, there are few people about, and the ones around are taking afternoon strolls as agreed by the government as part of the lock down regulations.

York is beautiful in the autumn afternoon sun, and they stroll hand in hand through the narrow streets, past the magnificent minster, down through Stonegate and Goodramgate.

They come across a small chapel off one of the main alleyways; the gate to the gardens and graveyard is open so they walk inside.

The grounds are beautifully tended, and as they approach the chapel, a gardener comes out, just as he is closing the large wooden door he beacons them in, "its quiet, no one inside if you would like to take a look around, I'm just having a break."

Churches were allowed to open, with restrictions in place for worship.

Sam and Liz entered the beautiful chapel, it was obviously very old, and the pews were still set in squares for family worship, as they would have done centuries ago.

The late sunlight danced through the magnificent stained glass windows, depicting religious scenes from the bible.

There were inscriptions set in the stone walls, of families who had worshiped there and were buried there.

As they walked around reading of the heritage of the people of York, they came upon a family tribute it was The Fencote family.

They read down the list of names, but one stood out more than the others

Jasper Fencote, 1630 to 1665, perished of the plague, is buried in the village of Hurworth.

"My god" said Sam, "that's where mum and dad live, that's amazing, we should try to research it."

They leave the chapel to its quiet emptiness, thanking the gardener on their way out.

On returning home, they settle down for the evening and turn on the computer to Face Time with Sam's Mum and Dad, his Mum is on screen, chatting about how well Liz is looking, telling her to enjoy this quiet time, as in a month there will be little time to relax.

As she speaks she is crocheting a beautiful lace shawl, in the finest of wool, there is love in every stitch and she proudly holds it up for Sam and Liz to see the progress.

Sam brings up the the name they had seen on the church wall, his Mum is visibly shaken, and goes quite pale, "are you sure Jasper Fencote?" she asks, "yes", replies Sam "why?"

When your father was coming out of his coma, he was quite delirious for some time, he spoke what seemed a load of nonsense at the time, but one name he repeated many times was Jasper Fencote.

"I have often asked him why, but he doesn't remember. I only know the name was spoken with anger."

At this point Tom comes into view on the screen, he smiles to greet them both, when they ask about Jasper Fencote, he looks blank, no idea, he comments.

That night Tom tossed and turned in bed, despite the cool November night, sweat poured from him, soaking his nightwear, he cried out but Ellen could not wake him, he thrashed about crying "run Samuel, go to the Brothers."

Ellen eventually calmed him, as they sat upright in bed she asked if he could remember his nightmare, he paused and said he couldn't, all he felt at the time was fear and wanting to protect

Sam, "but you called him Samuel", Ellen said, "we have never called him that."

Tom could not explain the feelings of despair he was left with; he would speak to the doctor the next day.

Tom explained to his GP, the symptoms he was having, the night terrors and feelings of deja vu at random moments.

His doctor explained, that many people especially the more serious covid cases like his, were experiencing a condition called long covid, as the pandemic was new, little research had been done and there were many different forms, all producing different symptoms, he prescribed some anti-depressants and something to help him sleep.

Tom felt better, just talking about it, but there was still a niggling, doubt troubling him.

Over the next few weeks, talk of the up and coming birth of their granddaughter alleviated most of his symptoms, he was even sleeping better.

Ellen and Tom busied themselves, buying little gifts on line, it was so different from when they had their two sons, and everything had to be checked out with Sam and Liz for safety issues.

There were machines for everything now, ones to make up formula bottles, ones to sterilise everything, ones to put disposable nappies in.

Monitors to watch baby sleeping (or not).

It was all very educational, and they laughed together at the crazy ideas, but knew that Sam and Liz would be using all of them.

They made a little nursery at their house, for when the time would come when little one could visit, they filled it with bright coloured toys, bought a cot and bouncer on an auction site, but bought the mattress new, with bumpers to match the décor. They were like two birds nesting, so happy to be part of this amazing event.

Next time they were in contact with Sam and Liz they walked upstairs to show the baby's finished room, as they climbed the stairs Liz said, "apparently cot bumpers aren't safe", Tom flew into the room ahead of Ellen and the bumpers were removed before Liz had chance to see them. Liz could not understand the giggles from her in laws, but thanked them for the beautiful, perfect room.

Tom has taken to walking every day, to try to build up his strength.

There are some beautiful walks around the village, his favourite is down past the Ringfield, where the village kids sledge in the winter, then follow the river along the edge of the farm land, past the back of Rockcliffe Hall, a beautiful hotel and golf course, the hotel was formerly a hospital run by the Brothers of St John of God, and has been sympathetically restored to keep a lot of the original features.

He walks on past the training ground for Middlesbrough football club. He crosses the river over to Croft, where St Peters church sits majestically overlooking the river, in the 1840"s the rectors young son Charles Lutwidge Dodgson (better known as his subsequent pen name, Lewis Caroll) took much inspiration from artefacts in the church, which would later influence aspects of Alice in Wonderland, such as the grinning cat on the cedilla is said to have inspired his creation of the Cheshire Cat.

He walks on past The Croft Hotel, formerly known as The Croft Spa, built in 1835, to replicate the spa baths fed from a spa called "Canny Well" in the woods, it is believed that the well was found when workmen were boring for a local farmer, the water when analysed was found to contain a high amount of sulphur, which rivalled the Harrogate Spa.

People flocked from all over the country, to bathe and drink the water, which was said to alleviate rheumatism, gout and many other ailments.

Tom walked on past a large hall and into the woods beyond. For December is was a mild day and as he reached the old well, he paused to drink his water (though not from the well).

The day was bright and the sounds of the birds calmed him, he sat propped against a large oak tree, he closed his eyes and felt more relaxed than he had for a long time.

As he dozed in the afternoon sun something made him stir, it sounded like a baby's cry; he looked around expecting to see walkers, as this was quite a popular walk for dog walkers. There was no one in sight. Perhaps a fox cub or early flight of an owl, but no, there it was again, a definite baby's cry.

Puzzled he rose and headed back home, not too concerned, his mobile phone rang, it was Ellen, Liz had gone into labour early, they were rushing her to York hospital.

Tom upped his pace, knowing they would not be able to go to York, because of the restrictions, but needed to be home to support them in any way he could, as he reached the edge of the dense woodland he glanced to the side and noticed a couple standing under the big oak, holding a tiny baby, they were dressed in very dark clothes, but the baby was wrapped in the most beautiful shawl. Tom raised an arm in recognition and continued on his way; relieved his imagination was not running wild again.

When he arrived home, Ellen was frantic, the hospital were about to perform a caesarean section on Liz, as the baby was distressed.

Sam kept in contact, he would be allowed in to the delivery room in time for the little one to be born, it only took what seemed like minuets before a beautiful girl arrived, there were no complications, she was a healthy weight, she was washed and handed to Sam who beamed proudly at this wonderful sight before him, her little eyes bright as buttons staring at him, he kissed her little hands one by one, then embraced Liz who looked radiant.

Whilst Liz was having her wound stitched the nursing staff put Sam and the little one in an adjoining room, as she was born so quickly, she was a little cold so, normally they would have had skin to skin contact with mum, but Sam was asked to unbutton his shirt and hold the little one close to warm her, its was the most wonderful experience, one that he would never forget.

Sam sent a video to his mum and dad, who wept with relief at the sight of their new granddaughter.

"What will you call her?" they asked Sam and Liz, "we thought Ali might be nice", so it was agreed?

As Liz could not manage alone it was agreed with the hospital staff, that they could move back in with Tom and Ellen, until Liz was strong enough to cope, obviously this was not a problem to the proud grandparents.

Sam and Liz left the hospital the next day and travelled to Hurworth, where Tom and Ellen greeted them, they held baby Ali for the first time, and she was dressed in what Tom described as a growbag! But still looked adorable, they soon got them all settled in.

Later that evening when Tom and Ellen were in the baby's room, they were unpacking the little ones things and putting them in drawers, they came upon the crocheted shawl that Ellen had spent hours lovingly making, she held it up and commented, "apparently they don't wear shawls these days" "strange" said Tom, the baby in Spa woods today was wrapped in a lovely shawl, Ellen shook her head and gave him her usual quizzical look, and carried on folding tiny vests.

CHAPTER 11

Spa Woods – December 1665

Samuel and Elizabeth continue to live in the cosy shack they now see as home, the days are much shorter, and the weather closing in, but the log stove keeps them warm, and Samuel has layered the roof and walls with new timbers, which keeps out the rain and soon to be snow. The trees form a protective barrier from the outside world.

Before the plague hit, Elizabeth spent a lot of time in the kitchen of the big house with cook and Eleanor, so she was able to produce some tasty meals, out of the rabbits and trout, that Samuel caught and supplies they were given from the Brothers on a regular basis.

Elizabeth is growing tired, her belly seems to be extended as far as it will go, Samuel is concerned, his mother has sent linen and towels and all he will need, she has also sent a small book explaining childbirth.

He has seen most animals give birth, but fears that he will not be able to cope when the time comes.

It was early evening when Elizabeth started to have light pains, she walked through the first ones easily, Samuel built up the fire and put water on to boil, although according to the book it may take many hours before they were needed.

He walked with her and rubbed her back, they sat for a while then she lay on the bed.

Elizabeth drifted in and out of sleep for a few hours, until an excruciating pain ripped through her without warning. Samuel panicked, but although her frame was slight, Elizabeth bore the pains with great dignity, calculating when the next would come and breathed to calm her, Samuel gave her some of the potion the Brothers had advised for this stage.

After what seemed like hours, just as the sun was rising, the final stage came and with one almighty push a beautiful baby girl was delivered into the arms of Samuel, he gazed in wonder at this tiny form, and then remembered his duties, to cut the cord and wrap the little one in a blanket and hand her to Elizabeth, who despite the ordeal, was looking radiant.

Elizabeth was given more herbs and potions, and was soon able to feed the baby.

Samuel looked on in wonder, "what will we name her?" he asked, "Alice", replied Elizabeth, "that was my mother's name."

They heard rustling outside, at a safe distance the Brothers had come, it was as if they knew of the arrival, they blessed the little one and left gifts and a bottle of apple brandy, Samuel asked them to inform his parents and his Lordship of the safe arrival of baby Alice.

There was news from London, Parliament had returned to the capital, and with the onset of colder weather, cases of the plague were starting to fall, although even with this news Samuel decided it was too early to move back to the village, besides, he was quite happy with his new found family here.

Christmas was fast approaching, although there would be no celebrations or church services, Samuel made a garland of holly, ivy and mistletoe and hung it round the door of the shack, inside he placed sweet smelling herbs around the candles.

Snow stared to fall; the Brothers had brought provisions for the next few weeks, fearing they would not be able to get to them if the weather worsened.

There was a cooked goose, potatoes, turnips and a plum pudding. A small gift of a silver rattle for the little one.

Samuel carved two tiny dolls out of oak, and Elizabeth sewed dainty white dresses for the dolls out of some of her underwear. She made tiny garlands for their heads out of dried flowers.

Christmas morning brought heavy snow, which drifted around the shack; they had plenty of dry firewood and built up the fire for the day.

They busied themselves together preparing their Christmas feast, with baby Alice watching on from her crib, she was smiling now and found them very entertaining, singing carols as they worked.

The apple brandy was opened, and the delicious meal eaten, Samuel thought he had never been so happy, he knew the time was fast approaching when they would need to return to the village, but for today at least they would savour the moment.

The Lychgate, All Saints Church

Graveyard All Saints Church

Spring on The Green

Lane leading up from the river to the green

Village Green

Primroses

Canny Well, Spa Woods

Plaque on village green, in memory of the 1665 plague victims

The Emmy

CHAPTER 12

Hunworth Village – January 1666

The time had come to move back to the village, there had been no further deaths caused by the plague, although some of the elderly residents has passed away due to influenza and bronchitis brought on by the cold weather.

Elizabeth was to move back into the big house with her father and Samuel would go back home to work with his father.

Elizabeth presented her beautiful daughter for the first time to her father, his tears were happy tears, this little ray of sunshine in such a terrible time, was welcomed with open arms. Cook could not stop blubbering. Eleanor had returned to help at the big house and in turn held the baby; she was also filled with emotion.

Samuel and his father took up their blacksmith's duties, although there were far fewer horses now, there was still a lot of repair work to do, they helped at the big house where needed, Samuel spent as much time as possible with Elizabeth and Alice, he was determined to be there in any way he was needed, everyone realised that he and Elizabeth were inseparable now.

Thomas and Samuel visited the Brothers, they helped with repairs on the farmland and any other tasks required, their gratitude was accepted gracefully by the Brothers, not one of them had succumbed to the plague, they just continued to exist in the same simple way they had for years.

Winter turned to spring and the Village Green was once again, bordered by snowdrops and aconites, the mounds were less noticeable now, but a chilling sight to all who passed by.

The people of the village rallied together, they worked what land they could together, some new residents moved in from some of the larger towns, which brought a much needed workforce to renew what had been lost.

The ale house re-opened, and a small schoolhouse, although the numbers of children were far less. The sounds of children playing again were a joy to hear.

CHAPTER 13

May Day – 1666

May Day was always celebrated in the village; it had been banned in 1644 under the Puritan reformation, but re-instated in May 1660 when the monarchy was restored.

The May pole this year though was to be erected on the front lawn of the big house, leaving the village green to rest for another year.

The pole was decorated with spring flowers, and all the staff at the big house were given time off for the celebrations.

Cook and Eleanor busied themselves cooking and baking for everyone.

The weather was kind, a warm sunny day, the villagers held hands and danced around the pole, saying goodbye to more than the cold winter as tradition would have it, but events that had shaken the village to its core.

There was an air of hope, a new beginning, Samuel and Elizabeth proudly introduced baby Alice, and everyone adored her, and were happy to see the young couple together at last.

The Brothers came, bringing apple brandy and cider, the celebrations and merriment went on way into the night, the sounds of singing and dancing could be heard way into the distance.

Hurworth Village 2021

Covid is still with us, although the first covid vaccine was given in early December 2020, the roll out is taking time.

12th April 2021

Pubs were to re-open, albeit serving in outside areas only, there was a noted air of hope around.

CHAPTER 14

May Day – 2021

Tom and Ellen were at home; a Bank holiday was really not much different these days.

Sam and Liz had returned to York, so the house was quiet and after a quick video chat with Liz and baby Ali, they decided to put their boots on and have a walk.

Most restrictions had been lifted, so things seemed to be getting back to some kind of normality, they walked around the village down to the riverside and sat overlooking the stunning countryside, Tom decided that the Emmy would be open from lunchtime, so they sauntered back in that direction. Up the lane past the green Ellen stopped to talk to some friends on the way, it still looked strange to hold a conversation wearing masks and standing six feet apart.

Tom continued on towards the pub, at the top of the green he paused to see if Ellen was following, she waved him on, "get them in, I'll be there soon."

Tom turned to continue on his way, but heard music and laughter from behind the hedge of the big house, must be having a party he thought, restrictions had been lifted to thirty people at a gathering, and most families were starting to catch up after the harrowing year they had all gone through.

He peeped through the fence, what he saw was amazing, it was like a film set from years gone by, a May pole decorated with spring flowers and villagers in ancient costumes were dancing around it holding hands and singing. He looked around for film cameras; perhaps it was some kind of documentary on the old house.

He recognised the young couple with the baby he had seen in Spa woods recently, the little one was about the same age as Ali, he waved but they did not acknowledge him.

Tom walked away smiling, hopefully someone in the pub would know what was going on.

Ellen caught up with him, and they sat in the window overlooking the fields, the new crops were a welcome sight, swathes of green shoots swaying in the spring breeze. The spring lambs were now chubby and frolicking along the hedgerows of the fields, ducks with lines of babies swimming rapidly to catch up in the flowing river, a view they never tired of.

A few of the regulars had had the same idea and joined them. When Tom asked what was going on at the big house, they looked at him with the usual bemused expressions, by now Tom had quite a reputation for seeing things that no one else had, as usual Ellen shook her head and smiled, Tom though was not amused, he would go back and convince them all, by the time he returned to the pub, his face told them the garden was empty, it had felt so real though, and Tom agreed with Ellen, he needed to have another check up with the Long Covid team at the hospital.

Tom had his appointment at the hospital by telephone, an entirely new concept, which was becoming the norm, the Doctor assured him, his symptoms were quite normal and it would take time to recover completely, he was advised to take extra precautions, as the signs of covid rising again were causing concern, it was expected by November that cases would again reach pandemic numbers.

By summer 2021 there had been over 200,000 deaths in the UK alone, with worldwide deaths reaching over 6 million.

Toms father was a sprightly eighty-four-year old, living in a town close by, he would visit Tom and Ellen on a regular basis two or three times a week, he loved the village and was often seen walking around the green, which took him for ever as he would stop and sit on one of the benches talking to everyone that passed.

When he contracted covid, Tom and Ellen were concerned, he started with what seemed like a Summer cold, but soon was admitted to hospital with breathing difficulties he was kept in hospital for a few weeks but as the bed spaces were limited he was transferred to a care home to recuperate.

Tom and Ellen had not been allowed to visit, while he was in hospital, so hoped the move would allow more access. They were still not allowed to visit, and his father's health deteriorated, they could look through his bedroom window, but by now all expression had gone from his face and he passed away peacefully, the staff were with him, but Tom mourned the fact that he had not been able to hold him one last time, and tell him what a great father he was.

The funeral was limited to fifteen mourners, which made it an even sadder affair.

The village came out and lined the path up to the church, leaving the customary two metre gap between them, the doors of the church were left open and they joined in the singing, even non-believers would fail to be moved by the uplifting rendition of "How Great Thou Art"

The music crescendos over the fields as if lifting his soul over the village he loved.

'When through the woods, and forest glades I wander,
And hear the birds sing sweetly in the trees.
When I look down, from lofty mountain grandeur
And see the brook, and feel the gentle breeze.'

Tom did not cope well after the funeral, and he spent many hours just sitting on one of the benches on the village green, where his dad had spent many hours holding court with the locals, everyone who passed offered words of sympathy, one little one even placed a small posy of flowers by the leg of the bench, at this gesture Tom had to smile and remember his little granddaughter who had been so lucky to have such a wonderful great granddad, if only for a short while.

CHAPTER 15

York – 1666

Lord Fencote has restored his household, following the events of the plague, He still grieves the loss of his two sons Jasper and Henry to the sickness, his youngest Charles, now twenty had survived, but was unwilling to return to London where he had been studying before the plague.

The manor house had not seen visitors for some time, and now he felt it was time to start up the social gatherings that had been popular in times past.

Many invitations had been sent to the big house in Hurworth, but his Lordship had politely declined.

Lord Fencote was insulted by the negative responses, as he felt that he had always had a good relationship with the Lord and his family at Hurworth, so he decided to pay him a visit, sending a message stating that he and his son Charles would call while travelling North.

On receiving this news his Lordship consulted with Thomas, who was now employed as estate manager, leaving Samuel to run the blacksmiths.

Thomas had been expecting news of this kind, and advised his Lordship that they would welcome the Fencotes and explain that work on the estate had increased a great deal since the sickness, and would do their utmost to revive the past relationships the two families had.

Thomas was happy to be advisor to his Lordship, but this visit lay heavy on his mind.

The Fencotes arrived and were welcomed into the hall, where cook and Eleanor had prepared a hearty meal of roast beef.

Immediately Lord Fencote declared that he would like Thomas to take Charles under his wing, and teach him the skills of estate management, he offered a large sum of money to his Lordship in return for Thomas to teach Charles everything needed to run the estate, the farming, managing the labourers, the maintenance of the workers cottages and all the financial dealing that went alongside.

The big house had suffered during the past year and with Thomas's expertise had just started to move forward again, but finances were tight and the offer was too good for his Lordship to pass, so he, with Thomas's blessing, went ahead and agreed that for one year Charles would move into the Big House.

Charles was very quiet during the conversation, obviously this was not the future he had envisaged, the thought of working for a living repulsed him, but he knew his father's word was final, it was this or return to London, he reluctantly agreed.

Charles left the gentlemen to their wine and farming conversation and took a stroll outside he wandered aimlessly around the large gardens wondering how he was going to survive a year in this god forsaken house, in a village with one alehouse, he was so used to socialising in and around York, with his well-heeled friends.

On a bench in the garden Elizabeth sat watching baby Alice on a rug, the little one was playing with two tiny wooden dolls, beautifully carved from oak, they were dressed in white lace with garlands around their heads, Alice was just starting to crawl and explore every tiny flower and blade of grass. Elizabeth acknowledged him with a smile, but as he approached closer she recognised the familiar Fencote face, her blood ran cold as the memories of the past came flooding back, she bent to pick baby Alice up, but Charles sat down on the grass beside the baby. He smiled at the little one, who in turn giggled with delight at the attention. He introduced himself politely offering his hand, Elizabeth shook it and introduced herself as Elizabeth, the daughter of his Lordship. He had heard of Elizabeth, but seeing her for the first time he was stunned by her natural beauty.

Charles picked up the dolls and started to animate a ring of roses dance with them, which amused Alice enormously.

He chatted casually about what lay ahead, he confided in Elizabeth that he was not looking forward to moving to the village, and that farming was definitely not for him, but in his mind he was thinking, perhaps this wont be so bad after all.

Elizabeth excused herself and stood to pick up Alice, in a flash Charles had scooped up the little one lifting her high, with squeals of delight Alice and her dolls were placed ever so carefully back in her mother's arms.

Charles bade her farewell, taking a last look at Alice something caught his eye, her little face looked very familiar.

Samuel had heard of the visit by Fencote and Charles from Thomas, he was furious, but as usual Thomas calmed him assuring him that it was purely a business venture, they would treat Charles with respect and do all that was asked of them, but he did ask Samuel to keep away as much as possible to avoid any confrontation, as it was, no one else knew of the incident over a year ago, and that's how it should stay.

Samuel reluctantly agreed, but went off to see Elizabeth and baby Alice.

He caught up with them in the kitchen of the big house, Elizabeth was chatting to cook and Eleanor was holding Alice who had a wooden spoon in her hand, Samuel beamed with joy at the sight and motioned for Elizabeth to come outside to talk.

Samuel expressed his concerns about Charles moving in, but Elizabeth was quick to reassure him that she had no wish to even speak to Charles, she would stay as far away from him as possible.

Charles returned to York to pack up his belongings from the Manor house, as he walked through the large imposing house he found himself at the foot of the grand staircase, leading up to a gallery on the first floor, he wandered along the plush carpeted landing which was flanked with family portraits going back centuries, the imposing pictures were all beautifully framed, he knew the names of most of the relatives, and smiled at the familiar faces looking down on him.

One of the most recent portraits caught his eye, it was of his late brother Jasper when he was an infant, probably around nine months old, the setting was in a garden where he was seated with two spaniel puppies, his blond curls framing a cherub like face, that face was so much like Elizabeth's daughter Alice, the resemblance was uncanny.

The Big House

Charles and his manservant Scully drove the forty miles from York to Hurworth in a small coach, Charles' favourite horse Samson trotted along behind, a beautiful jet- black stallion, which he adored.

They pulled up at the Big House and were welcomed warmly by Thomas and his Lordship.

Samuel took the horses and settled them into the stables, he admired the beautiful Samson, who was not in the least bit spooked by his new surroundings, but nuzzled up to Samuel, who in turn stroked the silky soft hair around his mane.

Charles was shown to his rooms, an elegant room overlooking the gardens to the rear of the property, with a smaller annex for his manservant, he was quite surprised at this as, in his father's house the servants were all housed in much simpler accommodation.

Dinner was served in the large dining room, cook had prepared her usual fare, terrine of ham hock, game pie with parsnips and turnips, and a delicious desert of plums and apples in cider. Eleanor had stayed back to serve the guests, Charles felt she was a little reserved, but she was courteous and spoke only when required. The wine flowed and Charles warmed to this household, he retired, thanking his Lordship and Thomas.

Scully had eaten in the kitchen, he and cook had hit it off instantly, with tales of wealthy families know to both of them, they talked way into the night and Skully crept up to his bed just after midnight, cheeks glowing with the cider he and cook had shared, this household was certainly different to the Manor House, he would not miss the strict rules shouted to him by Lord Fencote.

Back in his room Charles relaxed and looked out at the evening sky, the sun just setting over the stunning countryside, this day was nearly over, what would tomorrow bring he wondered.

All thoughts disappeared as he settled into his comfortable bed, he felt at ease here today, he hoped the feeling would continue at least for a while.

The cock crowed as the first rays of sun hit the trees outside the bedroom window, Scully was already up and dressed, they descended the stairs together, Scully heading off to the kitchen, Charles to the dining room where Thomas greeted him, they breakfasted on ham and eggs before heading out to view the farmland.

The farm was big and sprawling, most of the close fields kept cattle and sheep, pigs were loose in the woodland with small sheds for shelter.

Further afield were crops of oats, barley and wheat, almost ready for harvesting.

An orchard filled with apples, pears and plums, the harvest this year would not be good, the spring had been a wet one and with few staff to tend the trees the yield would be smaller than usual.

There was a large walled kitchen garden, which was filled with vegetables and fruits, all planted carefully in tidy rows, this was cooks domain, but a few local lads would be available to do the heavy digging work.

Thomas and Charles headed for the stables, where Samuel had the horses saddled and ready, Charles thanked him, but Samuel just dropped his head and walked away, Thomas scowled at him, to no effect.

They rode out past the orchard and along the hedgerows lining the crop fields, the bushes were beginning to fill with berries, and wild birds flew up as they disturbed their feasting, blackbirds, thrush, chaffinch and fieldfare. Magpies jumped in and out of the longer grass.

Surprisingly the crops were doing much better than expected, the lack of seed earlier, following the plague, had led to smaller fields being sown, but in turn the crops were tended well by the smaller work force.

Thomas was confident that the harvest would be enough to sustain the farm for another winter, with some left to sell to the local miller.

Thomas explained the rotation system they used, to ensure the best yields, Charles surprisingly, found his experience fascinating, and asked many questions.

They rode around the bounds of the farmland, returning to the big house, Samuel by now was busy at the blacksmiths, but Skully tended the horses (although not as efficiently as other stable lads)

After lunch Thomas took Charles to check on the pigs, one of the sows was due to give birth, when they arrived, she was lying on her side with twelve piglets noisily clutching her teats, a relief to Thomas, within weeks they would go to market, bringing in a much-needed income.

They cleaned out the sty and left new bedding and water, with a few apples, and scraps from the kitchen.

Although Charles had never mucked out a farm animal before, he found it satisfying to see the sow nestled in her new bed with her babies.

Charles walked back to the house via the kitchen garden where cook and Skully were collecting vegetables for the evening meal, summer was coming to a close, but the garden was bountiful with plenty of produce to eat fresh or preserve for later, he picked a handful of pea pods and shelled them as he walked, they were as sweet as strawberries.

Cook gave him a welcoming smile, he complimented her on the array of produce, she said it was good to have Skully as an extra pair of hands, they seemed to be getting along well, and Charles agreed that cook was to use his manservant for any extra work she needed, Skully grinned a wide grin, and continued picking cabbages.

On approaching the house, he caught a glimpse of Elizabeth, he hurried to catch up with her but as he rounded the corner, Samuel was approaching, not wanting to encounter another cold shoulder, he turned and entered through the rear of the house.

Samuel and Elizabeth walked hand in hand through the gardens, baby Alice was asleep in the kitchen, with Eleanor looking on.

Elizabeth commented how charming Charles had been, but Samuel replied, "the sooner he is gone the better". Elizabeth felt him bristle at the name of Fencote and left the conversation well alone for now.

The Autumn months passed, Charles was kept busy with Thomas, he enjoyed the work, Thomas was a good teacher and very patient when Charles had difficulties understanding even the simplest of tasks.

Samuel stayed away but the time was coming when Thomas needed him to teach Charles the running of the Blacksmiths.

The first day at the smithy, Samuel set Charles to use the large bellows to heat the fire to make the metal soft enough to work.

The heat was incredible, and Charles struggled to keep up, Samuel smirked at his pathetic effort, luckily Thomas called by, and Samuel allowed Charles a break to catch his breath, the scowl on Thomas's face told Samuel he would need to be more patient, his respect for his father, far outweighed any negative feelings he had for this intruder.

Samuel gradually allowed Charles to watch and then even hammer out a horseshoe, although it was not perfect, Charles asked Samuel if he could keep it, his sense of achievement bursting in his chest, Samuel agreed, and polished it, smiling at the strange request.

From then on, the relationship became less strained, and Samuel like his father was a good teacher, before long Charles was developing muscles like Samuel, and tackling larger tasks, between them they made a good team, Thomas would look on and smile as he watched them form a metal ring around a cartwheel together, hammering alternate strokes with such accuracy. He didn't notice Samuels firm grip on the hammer, his white knuckles as memories and regrets came flooding back.

CHAPTER 16

Hurworth Autumn – 2021

As winter approaches, more doom and gloom hits, there is a new variant of covid – Omicron is prevalent worldwide and in the UK, travel restrictions in and out of the county are back in place, facemasks compulsory once more in supermarkets and on public transport. The public are being advised to have booster jabs.

There has been talk of Ministers, breaking the covid rules and holding parties, many have been issued with fines of up to £200.00.

Tom wished he had broken the rules, just to have the chance to be with his father one last time, he would have broken the door down and gladly paid the consequence's.

Tom and Ellen are preparing for baby Ali's first birthday, Government advise that three households can form a bubble, so they have decided to have Ali and her Mum and Dad to stay with them over the Christmas period, there is talk of bigger lockdowns yet again after the festive season.

The Emmy is open, but restrictions are in place, only barmaid service, with no approaching the bar, face masks are to be worn when standing or moving around, some dividing panels have been placed on larger tables, minimising the numbers to four.

Tom and Ellen still pop in occasionally, but have given it a miss this week as they do not want baby Ali to be exposed to any infections.

They all settle down, cosy in the house, its lovely for Tom and Ellen to spend this precious time with the little one, they do worry though as Ali has had no contact with health visitors, all consultations are on line, and for the new parents it has been a very daunting time.

Sam and Liz feel re-assured by staying with Sam's parents.

During the second week of their stay, Ali has been off her food, she is very clingy with her mum and just not settling, when her temperature rises, alarm bells start to ring and Ellen phones 111, the medical staff advise keeping her cool and giving water, but to call back if her temperature does not drop, Ali continues to deteriorate, Ellen calls the helpline again, while Liz is talking to the hospital, Ali goes limp in Ellen's arms, she screams at the phone "she's not responding", the hospital says help is on the way.

Ellen's natural reaction is to slap little one on the back, at this she coughs and vomits, but is still struggling, Tom sits on the bottom stair in the hallway, he cant believe what is happening, he feels helpless.

A paramedic arrives, and checks baby Ali, who is now screaming at the sight of this alien with a mask, bearing in mind the only faces she has seen in her short life have been family ones.

"It's a good sign" says the paramedic, "but her temperature is high so we will need to take her to hospital, only mum will be allowed to go with her", the ambulance arrives an hour later, by which time Ali has calmed down,

Ali spent the night in The Memorial, she was allowed home the next day, it was explained to them that babies cannot regulate their own temperature, so the body's natural reaction is to close down, hence the traumatic reaction. Luckily, she had no adverse effects and made a quick recovery, however Tom took the incident badly, his night terrors returned.

He dreamt of a young lady with a baby, being lowered into a grave on the village green, he woke in a cold sweat, with Ellen holding him tightly.

Christmas passes, the family have enjoyed a peaceful time, and Sam and Liz decide it is time to return to York, they ask Tom and Ellen to come and stay for a while but Tom declines, he is still struggling and Ellen has become more worried about his behaviour, he goes for long walks on his own, and spends much time in bed, she fears his depression is worsening and pleads with him to seek a second opinion.

He says he's fine, but deep down she knows all is not well.

Tom's walks usually take him through the village down to the woods across the river,

As Tom walks on he cannot help but feel uplifted at the sight of the winter countryside, the willow trees branches dipping low to the ground beside the river, heavy with frost and icicles.

Ducks skate when landing on the frozen surface, the sun glints on the landscape and Tom thinks, later we'll go to the Emmy the view is stunning from there.

His thought are disturbed by a tiny voice, "hello" said the little one who had appeared out of nowhere, she stood by a fallen tree trunk, she held two tiny dolls and was making them dance on the flat surface of the tree stump. Tom looked around and could see no-one else, Tom replied "hello, where's your mummy?" "Mamas over there," Tom looked to see a beautiful young lady approaching, she was dressed in an elegant cloak, edged with fur, he nodded in greeting and touched his cap, he felt as if he was in the presence of some aristocratic lady, but had no clue of who she was, the lady smiled, "you have a beautiful daughter," he said, "she is very like my own granddaughter, about the same age", the lady thanked him and took the little ones hand, as she started to walk away, the little one ran back to Tom and placed one of the dolls ever so carefully in his hand, he stared down at this beautiful object, and when he looked up again the lady and daughter had gone.

Tom felt uplifted, and headed for home, when he arrived back at the house he threw his arms around Ellen, "come on love, were going to the pub", she looked on in amazement, thinking (has he had one already) but gladly put on her coat and boots and headed for the Emmy.

Tom didn't mention his meeting in the woods today, he had learned to keep these episodes to himself.

They sat talking and laughing with friends well into the night, albeit through a Perspex screen, perhaps this was life now Tom thought and ordered another pint of Guinness.

At closing time, they both had a bit of a wobble walking down the lane to home, the night was stunning, frosty with clear starry skies, a shooting star flashed above them and they both caught a glimpse of it, Tom kissed Ellen on the cheek.

After a struggle with the front door key, Ellen helped Tom off with his coat, he poured them both a drink while Ellen hung up his coat, she missed the peg first time and giggled like a school girl, much to Toms amusement, on the second attempt she managed and smoothed the fabric lovingly, she felt something in the pocket and when she looked it was a tiny wooden doll dressed in an exquisite lace dress with garlands around her head, she placed it back not saying a word.

CHAPTER 17

Hunworth - Spring 1667

Samuel and Charles have been working well together, Charles has convinced Samuel that he is only there to work, with no intentions at all towards Elizabeth. Alice is now running about the estate, Samuel adores her and spends as much time as he can with her, she has her own little hammer and she bangs large logs in time with Samuel and Charles, closely watched by Elizabeth or Eleanor. Charles is planning a visit to York, his father is hosting a Spring Ball, he is trying to persuade Samuel and Elizabeth to join him, Elizabeth is dying to go but Samuel is reluctant, but agrees as he knows Elizabeth will only go without him.

Elizabeth is so excited, it has been years since she attended such an event, Eleanor helps with choosing fabric for a new gown, his Lordship will find suitable attire for Samuel, but refuses to join them in York.

Eleanor has agreed to move into the big house to look after Alice until they return, cook is looking forward to the reduction in work for a few days, they have kept it quiet but Skully has proposed, they will wait until the party returns before they announce the news.

Elizabeth will ride in the coach with Samuel, Skully will drive and Charles will ride Samson alongside. They set off early in the morning, it was a long journey ahead.

As they journeyed through the countryside they passed through small villages, most of the road was well travelled but parts still took them through dense woodland, it was in one of these that three horsemen barred the way telling Skully to stop, they held pistols, Skully knew at once they were highwaymen, since the plague there had been an increase in robberies along this road.

Charles was quite a way behind, but managed to see what was happening and rode into the woods to try to get ahead of them. Samuel jumped out of the carriage but was struck immediately by one of the robbers with the butt of his pistol, Elizabeth was terrified, they demanded her valuables, as they were busy rifling through the bags, Charles appeared out of nowhere, he was brandishing a pistol and fired a shot into the air, "put the bags down or I will shoot", he shouted, they did as asked and backed away, the robbers re-mounted and started to ride away, Charles made chase but one of them turned and fired, the shot hit Sampson and he and the horse fell to the ground. Samuel managed to stand, his head wound was slight and he ran to Charles who was just standing up, the shot had missed him but hit Sampson in the flank, the horse lay on the ground and Charles placed his pistol on the horses forehead, "no" said Samuel, "I think I can help him."

Taking one of the coach horses he rode at speed back to the Brothers, they came with a cart and winch and loaded the poor animal onto it.

Samuel told Charles to carry on to York, the Brothers had sent men to accompany them, they were less likely to be attacked it there were men of the cloth present, he would return to the big house and try to save Sampson, Charles was still in shock and agreed, but in his heart felt it would be the last time he would see his beloved horse.

With the help of farmworkers, Samuel got Sampson back to the stable, the large horse was sweating profusely and his large black eyes stared in fear and pain, at once Samuel knew to use the herbal remedies that the Brothers used, he would calm the wound before removing the shot. He slept beside the horse all night, and by morning Samson was calm enough for him to remove the shot, he cleaned and dressed the wound, although still unable to stand the horse made steady progress throughout the day. Samuel had never owned a horse before, but had such feelings for this beautiful animal, the horse in turn trusted Samuel and together they fought for the horses' survival.

York 1667
Fencote Manor

The day of the Spring Ball was approaching, Elizabeth was made very welcome by Lord Fencote, and enjoyed the hustle and bustle of preparations, Charles had impressed his father with his new found farming knowledge, and although Lord Fencote was not a man to issue compliments readily, he took time to listen to Charles and they discussed how they would move forward with the estate, using the same methods that The Big House had used for years. Charles for once felt the respect and admiration from his father, he had always wanted to please him, but was rebuked as being too young and inexperienced, a bit of a day dreamer. As the only surviving son, he had now proved his rightful place in the family.

Elizabeth spent the days leading up to the ball helping the household staff, they loved her and were more than happy to give her free reign in the decorations and menu choices, Lord Fencote was enchanted with her, and many times asked Charles why he was not spending more time with this beauty, Charles replied that she was taken, but said no more. Lord Fencote decided to speak to Skully to try to find out who the lucky gentleman was, and when he found out that it was Samuel a local blacksmith, he was not amused, he was determined that Charles would wed Elizabeth.

One day when Elizabeth was wandering around the great manor, she too came upon the family portrait gallery, and as had Charles, was amazed at the painting of the young Jasper, the features, the blonde curls even the shape of lips were identical, she shuddered at the memory of what happened two years ago, she didn't hear Charles approaching, and was startled to turn and see him behind her, he placed a gentle hand on her shoulder, she wondered if he too had realized, but he said nothing, just gently lead her away down the staircase.

A rider was sent to say Samuel would not be attending the ball, he explained to Charles, that although he had removed the shot, Sampson was still weak, and unable to stand, the next few days would be crucial if he was to survive. Elizabeth was not surprised, she knew he would not feel comfortable in these surrounding, however she intended to stay and make the most of it, she sent a message back stating she hoped he was well and she and Charles would return after the ball.

The night of the ball finally arrived, there were Lords and Ladies from far and wide, some had even travelled from London, it was to be the highlight of the social year, and everyone was in high spirits. Lord Fencote welcomed them into his beautiful manor house, which Elizabeth had decorated exquisitely with spring blossoms and trailing foliage, his Lordship had never seen the house looking so beautiful, since the passing of his wife, he had no interest in his surroundings, but he was seeing it as if for the first time, and thanked Elizabeth, hinting that it all could be hers one day, if she were to marry Charles, Elizabeth blushed and excused herself, she hurried away before any further comments could be made, Lord Fencote busied himself with his guests who were enjoying the hospitality immensely.

The food, wine and merriment carried on way into the small hours, Elizabeth happily danced with many of the young gentlemen, she felt as if she was back at the big house before the sickness, when they would hold such balls, although not quite as elaborate. She remembered as a young girl dancing with her father, it made her quite homesick, and was looking forward to the next day when she and Charles would return.

As the night was drawing to a close, Charles requested the last dance from Elizabeth, she accepted gracefully, it was a slow dance and Charles held her gently but firmly, Lord Fencote looked on and smiled, perhaps she may be persuaded to change her mind, especially if the young blacksmith was out of the picture.

The following day, the coach was packed up and Elizabeth and Charles were awaiting Skully, he had been in a meeting with Lord Fencote and came to the coach ashen faced, he whipped the horses into action and didn't speak all the way back to Hurworth. Elizabeth had a bad feeling, but Charles knew his scheming father and would speak to Skully later.

Back at the big house, Samuel had managed to get Samson to eat, he was growing stronger and making attempts to get up, but still struggling, even with two farm hands to support him he would still collapse back onto the soft straw. Samuel knew if he couldn't stand he would have to be shot, at that moment the coach pulled up and Charles instantly ran to the stables, he was so distressed to see his beautiful horse trying so hard, Samuel was making one last attempt to stand him up, Charles went to the other side of the horse and between them they managed to get him upright, he was unsteady at first but soon was standing unaided. Without any thought,

Charles threw his arms around Samuel, words would not come as tears streamed down his face. His reaction stunned Samuel, who was just as emotional at the sight of Samson nuzzling between them both.

Samuel left the stables to greet Elizabeth, his mother Eleanor had brought little Alice out to welcome her back, Elizabeth was overjoyed to see the little one, she seemed to have grown in the few weeks she had been in York, Eleanor explained she had been fine, although had spent a lot time with Samuel and Samson, Thomas had made her a little hobby horse with a black head, and she called it Sammy and would pretend to ride around the grounds. Samuel hugged Elizabeth, so glad to have her back, she held him closely, not caring who would see. Charles looked on from the stables and smiled.

CHAPTER 18

Hurworth – March 2022

All covid restrictions have now been lifted, however the cases are still rising, although most people have had all their vaccination's plus booster jabs, it appears that this is how the country will move forward.

Schools have re-opened, bringing more cases of childhood illnesses as little ones mix again for the first time. Their immune systems have not had to deal with common viruses, over the lock down periods, scarlet fever, which has not been common for years now, is suddenly on the increase, as is Strep A, which although quite common can be quite serious, it's a worrying time for parents.

Sam and Liz have both returned to work, Alice is at nursery, but Tom and Ellen go to York to look after her for two days in the week.

They love to take her out and explore, the historic town is fascinating and they find something new to do every week.

Tom and Ellen's youngest son Charlie, lives and works in London, he doesn't get home very often, but is planning to have his upcoming wedding in the summer back home in the village.

It will be a quiet occasion, with a small church service and a reception in Hurworth Grange, the local community centre, which is well equipped for such occasions.

His parents have been given the task of organising everything, which they are happy to do, in fact they are thrilled to be able to busy themselves, although challenging they throw everything they have at it, to ensure it will be a memorable day.

Ali will be a bridesmaid, and Ellen spends many hours looking for the perfect dress, she finds one in a bespoke wedding outfitter in York, creamy, white lace in a ballerina style with tiny ballet pumps to match.

Ali loves the dress and prances around the dress shop, complaining "not yet" when she had to take it off.

Charlie and his wife Sarah, although living in London, love the chance to come back to the village for a break from the hustle and bustle of city life, they request that Ellen and Tom keep the preparations as simple as possible, which is fine, Ellen has already ordered a homemade buffet from the landlady of a small pub at the edge of the village, a friend will make a tower of cupcakes as a wedding cake, and when Sainsbury's have the special offer on champagne they will purchase a fair amount.

Liz is very creative, and has many ideas for decorating the big room at the Grange, wildflowers will be used for centre pieces, with tubs of roses planted on the patio areas outside. There will be entertainment for the smaller children, and a local band will provide music for the evening. Lanterns and candles will be placed around the outside spaces.

It was to be a typical village wedding, costing a fraction of the price that a big do would in London. Most of the guests would be family and friends from the village, with a few of Sarah's' relatives staying at the prestigious Rockcliffe Hall.

This is exactly what Charlie and Sarah dreamt of and were so grateful to Tom and Ellen for all of their hard work.

CHAPTER 19

The Big House – Spring 1667

The time for Charles to return to York, is almost here, he has gained so much knowledge, and feels confident in taking on the role of estate manager for Fencote Manor, he and Samuel had become quite close since Samson's injury, and spent much time together both in work and socially. Samuel will miss him, but will miss Sampson more, since they brought him back Charles has allowed Samuel to ride him, whenever he needed to, and loved to see them riding around the local area.

On his last day at the big house, Charles suggests they go to the local ale house one last time, they have asked Skully to join them, which he does reluctantly, since returning from Fencote Manor he has been withdrawn and Charles has feared that he may be ill, as yet he has not popped the question of marriage to cook, something seems to be praying on his conscience.

They drink into the small hours, and stagger back in good spirits.

The next morning Skully as usual is up and about before everyone, he has suggested that Samuel accompany them to York, perhaps as a safeguard against robbers, Samuel agrees and Skully suggests that he ride Sampson, Charles a little worse for wear after the previous evening, is happy to ride in the coach with Skully driving.

The day is clear and bright, and they make good progress, just before they see the majestical minster come into view, there is a skirmish ahead and two constables ride up, they grab the reins from Samuel, confused he looks to Skully who shouts, "that's him, he's stolen Lord Fencotes horse."

Samuel realises exactly what is going on and despite his protests of innocence realised he is in deep trouble. The constables lead him away to the prison in York where he will be tried by the Magistrate, if found guilty, he will be hanged.

Charles has slept through the whole incident and only wakes when they arrive at Fencote Manor. As he leaves the coach, he sees Skully leading Sampson into the the stables, "where is Samuel?" he asks, "oh, he has returned to Hurworth", replied Skully.

Lord Fencote, is beaming with the outcome, he calls Skully and offers him his payment, Skully refuses to accept the large sum of money and says he is leaving. Lord Fencote shrugs and walks away, his plan is nearly complete.

Skully starts to head back to Hurworth, his feeling of betrayal overwhelming him with every step, how can he face Miss Elizabeth.

He decides to confide in Charles and meets him in the stables as he is tending Sampson, Charles is consumed with anger and heads straight for the manor, when he confronts his father, he is met with the stern face that he has not seen for many months, "it is for the best" his father explains, it is obvious that you and Elizabeth should be together, the child must be Jaspers".

Charles cannot comprehend what his father is saying, and says he will go to the Magistrate and explain that he gave permission for Samuel to take the horse he prays he will not be too late.

Skully has made his way back to Hurworth, he hopes that Thomas will be able to help, as he explains, he breaks down, he says he will do anything to rectify his wrong doing, but fears it may be too late.

Thomas can understand how manipulative Lord Fencote is, and thanks Skully for coming back, he wastes no time in contacting the Brothers, if he can prove that Samuel is of good character, they make be able to save him.

The head of the order, accompanies Thomas at speed on the trip to York, they arrive in the early evening at the prison in York, the magistrate has left for the day, the prison guard bows to the brother and allows him and Thomas to pass, they walk to the cell where Samuel is held, he sits with his head in hands, when he sees his father he cannot hold his emotion and weeps, Thomas assures him all will be well, they will stay till morning and plead with the magistrate.

At the first light the sounds of hooves wake them from their slumber, Charles has ridden to the prison on Samson. He dismounts just as the Magistrate is arriving, they are all beckoned into a large chamber, the Magistrate declares how serious the offence is and asks what defence they can give, the head brother starts first and explains how he has seen Samuel grow from a small child, the help that he and his father had given the order was beyond any other.

The Magistrate has heard of his Lordship in Hurworth, a much-respected pillar of the community. The order of Brothers were well known for their good work within the surrounding areas, his own family had been helped by them during the plague and he thanked him for his kindness.

Charles speaks next and explains to the learned gentleman about Samuel saving Samson's life after robbers attacked them, he says he owed much to the father and son who had taken him in and taught him the skills he now had, he explained that he had given permission for Samuel to ride Sampson whenever he saw fit, and asked the Magistrate to bring Samuel outside, this was reluctantly agreed, but as soon as Sampson saw Samuel he whinnied and placed his head against the blacksmiths broad chest, it was obvious that the horse had a special fondness for Samuel.

Thomas could only plead as a father, he wept as he begged for leniency.

The Magistrate placed a hand on Samuels shoulder and pardoned him, he was free to go.

Thomas wanted to go straight to Fencote Manor but Charles advised that he would speak to his father, he said if his father would not apologise he would have nothing more to do with him. He knew he would be giving up his inheritance, but could not stand by and let his father rule over him again.

Charles would explain to his father that he had no intention of marrying Elizabeth and if Fencote Manor were to have any future whatsoever, they would need to work together, the Magistrate agreed not to prosecute Lord Fencote as long as he made good to all concerned.

Samuel and Thomas along with the brother left York and headed back to Hurworth.

Skully sat in the kitchen of the big house, he had never felt so desolate, for once in his life he had found happiness and now Lord Fencote with his evil ways had ruined any chance of it.

His Lordship had news from York that Samuel had been pardoned and eagerly awaited his return, Elizabeth hugged her father and Alice played on the kitchen floor, oblivious to the goings on.

Cook and Eleanor prepared for the return of the men, they cooked a supper of game pie and turnips, his Lordship asked cook to bring up a special wine as he had an announcement to make that evening.

Thomas and Samuel entered the Big House through the kitchen, but his Lordship beckoned them into the large formal dining room

As they settled down to a hearty meal, all thoughts of the past few days gradually evaporated, his Lordship raised his glass and stated, "I am old now and feel my time is short, I would like to pass on the estate to my daughter Elizabeth, on the condition that she marries Samuel, I would ask Thomas to take over the running of the estate, with Samuel by his side I know they will care for the Big House as I have."

In the kitchen cook and Skully were making their own plans, Skully went down on one knee and proposed, cook accepted, at that Elizabeth burst in and declared, lets have a joint wedding.

Back in York at Fencote Manor Charles and his father agreed to try to make things work, they drew up plans for the new running of the estate, Lord Fencote was a beaten man, and accepted that Charles was more than capable of overseeing the changes, he agreed to everything.

Later that evening Charles alighted the stairs to the portrait gallery to find his father staring at the portrait of Jasper as an infant, he sobbed as he had when he visited the burial mounds at Hurworth, Charles held his father close for the first time, "I know" he said "I know."

CHAPTER 20

All Saints Church, Hurworth – Summer 2022

It's a beautiful sunny day, the sky is bright blue with soft billowing clouds above the fields adjoining the church.

Sarah looking stunning in an elegant cream gown makes her way through the Lychgate around to the main entrance to the church, on the arm of her father she stops to admire the beautiful flowers that have been woven with foliage around the ancient woodwork. Ali is hopping from one foot to the other, she cannot contain her excitement and Ellen has to put a finger to her lips to calm her, she clutches a posy of wild blooms, daisies, blue thistle and cow parsley.

Tom is inside with Charlie, he struggles to hold back the tears as he sees the bride appear, but smiles at Ali who is stealing the limelight as always.

Ellen steps in the pew beside Tom, she holds his hand, the church as always holds so many memories, some happy, some sad but always a feeling of complete calm.

After the service the congregation step outside, photographs are taken and friends and family start to make their way up to the Grange for the reception, Tom and Ellen walk through the churchyard, its always serene but today seems more so, they take Ali's little posy and lay it on Toms' dads grave, they stand in silence, both wishing he could have been here to see this special day.

They look out over the river to the fields beyond,

Sam calls to them, asking of they need a lift, Ali is playing up so Tom says he will walk up with her, but says for Ellen to go with them, (those shoes will never make it)

Tom and Ali hold hands as she dances out of the churchyard, they pass by a couple of the big houses, and make their way across the village green.

CHAPTER 21

The Big House – Summer 1667

His Lordship is standing in the hallway of the Big House, as Elizabeth slowly walks down the staircase, his eyes fill with tears, she looks just like her mother did on their wedding day all those years ago, the elegant cream lace dress is simple but stunning, she carries a small posy of summer flowers, cow parsley, blue thistle and daisies.

Alice skips behind her, looking so pretty in her little cream dress with matching shoes and garlands in her hair.

Samuel meets her at the small church, all the village are there to greet them, Thomas and Eleanor walk proudly behind and Alice walks between them holding hands and jumping.

The service is short and all are welcomed back to the big house for the wedding breakfast, cook and Skully despite their own wedding are busying looking after everyone.

Samuel has never looked so happy, and as they start their married life the bells toll out across the fields.

Thomas and Eleanor head back to the big house, Alice has stopped on the green to pick flowers, Thomas smiles at Eleanor and says he will catch up, "this may take some time" he smiles.

Tom and Ali walk slowly across the green, Thomas and Alice walk towards them, both girls are holding flowers and each has a small wooden doll clutched in a hand, the gentlemen smile at each other, admiring the girls similar dress and garlands, "wedding for you too?" says Tom, "Aye sir" says Thomas, they acknowledge each other with a strange recognition, the girls by now are holding hands and dancing around "ring a ring of roses" they sing.

The girls part and the men walk in opposite directions, as each look back the other is nowhere to be seen.